To read more about Stanley, look out for all the
Something Wickedly Weird books:

The Werewolf and the Ibis
The Ice Pirates
The Buccaneer's Bones
The Curse of the Wolf
The Smugglers' Secret
The Golden Labyrinth

Read more spooky tales in Dust 'n' Bones,
also by the award-winning Chris Mould.

And visit Chris at his website:
www.chrismouldink.com

THE SMUGGLERS' SECRET

CHRIS MOULD

*Hodder
Children's
Books*

A division of Hachette Children's Books

For my mother – Marvellous Margaret

Text and illustrations copyright © 2008 Chris Mould

First published in Great Britain in 2008
by Hodder Children's Books
This paperback edition published 2010

The right of Chris Mould to be identified as the Author and Illustrator
of the Work has been asserted by him in accordance with the
Copyright, Designs and Patents Act 1988.

1

A Catalogue record for this book is available from the British Library

ISBN 978 0 340 98920 3

Printed and bound in the UK by
CPI Bookmarque Ltd, Croydon, CR0 4TD

The paper and board used in this paperback by Hodder Children's Books
are natural recyclable products made from wood grown in sustainable
forests. The manufacturing processes conform to the environmental
regulations of the country of origin.

Hodder Children's Books
A division of Hachette Children's Books
338 Euston Road, London NW1 3BH
An Hachette UK company
www.hachette.co.uk

Admiral Buggles

A   The Wooden Mile
B   The Lighthouse
C   The Village Hall
D   Candlestick Hall
E   The Candle Shop
F   The Old Darkling Place
G   The Village Square
H   The Harbour
I   The Moor

Crampton Rock

An Old Flame

Night was drawing in on the island of
Crampton Rock. The fishermen had finished
work for the day and the harbour was
emptying slowly. But some stranger's boat
was approaching in the lost light. An oil
lamp hung off the bow and the small yellow
glow spread itself across the rippling water
ahead.

A frail hunched man in ragged clothes readied himself as the boat careered up to the harbour. He threw a length of wizened rope on to the nearest post and wound himself in.

Turning to his passenger, he gestured with a long bony finger to Candlestick Hall. 'That's it, sir. That's the old place. I heard it's a young lad that lives there now. Stanley Buggles. Inherited it from his great-uncle.'

'That don't sound right,' the passenger said gruffly. 'I ain't looking for no young lad. Still, it's late. Better take a look.'

'Are yer sure, sir? Strange place, this island. Ain't nowhere to be out in the dark, that's for sure.'

'Ahh, not to worry. It'll take more than a black night to frighten old MacDowell.'

The passenger gathered his things and made his way towards the Hall. Darkness had

blotted out
Crampton Rock and
the street lamps were all
that was left to show of the village.

A large pair of feet arrived on the steps of
Candlestick Hall and a skinny hand reached
for the door knocker. BANG, BANG, BANG.

*

Stanley did not like night-time visitors. They reminded him of the sinister arrivals he had had in the past. Pirates were the scourge of the Rock, and Stanley had had his fill of them. And then there were the Darklings, the strange family from the village who had recently tried to lay claim to his house, insisting that it was rightfully theirs. Edmund Darkling had plotted to be rid of young Stanley, and right now was awaiting trial for attempted murder.

Stanley's heart picked up pace and fluttered anxiously as he perched in front of the scullery fire. He knew a knock at this hour meant something out of the ordinary.

His trusty housekeeper Mrs Carelli clomped across the floorboards, and her husband Victor poked an inquisitive head around the door and peered into the hallway. Both were fiercely loyal to Stanley and would not allow anyone or anything to put him at risk.

'Who on earth is that at this time?' Victor wondered with a raised eyebrow.

Stanley chased up behind Mrs Carelli and prepared himself. His best punch was curled up neatly behind his back, and he was ready to leap in front of her.

The familiar creak of the door announced its opening.

'Aah, good evening there madam, young sir, my name is MacDowell and I be lookin' for a good friend o' mine.

Goes by the name o' Bartholomew Swift. I had a feelin' I was in the right place but something tells me I've taken a wrong turn.'

The newcomer was ragged and thin and wore a tattered patch over his left eye. A broad hat held on to trails of greasy unkempt hair and a spiky chin of grey tufts showed that he hadn't shaved for a while. A large gold earring hung from one lobe. He carried a modest bag of belongings over his shoulder and wore a droopy-eyed expression.

A shocked silence fell upon Stanley and Mrs Carelli, and Victor meandered slowly across the hallway to stand beside them. They all knew that any old friend of Stanley's great-uncle, Admiral Swift, would either be a naval man or a buccaneer. And by the look of him it was more than likely that he had a skull and crossbones tattooed somewhere about his loose-limbed body.

Stanley peered down. Stripy leggings were wrapped around bony legs and a pair of huge buckled shoes stuck out awkwardly at the ends.

'Ah, not to worry. I 'ad a feelin' I was in the wrong place. Doesn't matter. I apologize for disturbin' yer evenin'.'

The man began to wander down the path. The three looked at each other and hesitated. They knew nothing of this odd-looking stranger. What if he was a genuine good friend of Stanley's Great-Uncle Bart, the man who had died and left him his every possession?

Could they really turn him away?

'Stop!' cried Stanley.

'Stanley, no. Yer can't. We don't know him,' urged Mrs Carelli in a whisper that was so loud it could have woken the dead admiral.

MacDowell stopped and turned.

'Wait,' called Stanley. 'You haven't given us chance to explain. Bring your things and come inside. If nothing else, you need an explanation and a room for the night.'

'Are yer sure now? An old stranger like me? I could be anyone!'

'Come on,' urged Stanley further.

'Don't make me regret this, Stanley,' continued Mrs Carelli in his ear.

'Come and sit by the fire,' Victor said. 'We have much to tell you.'

The stranger shuffled into the house and they sat, all four of them, around the burning logs. They explained the dreadful circumstances of Admiral Swift's death at the curse of the werewolf, and how it had led to Stanley inheriting the old place, with Mr and Mrs Carelli alongside him.

MacDowell held his face in his hands. 'Me ol' mate Swifty. We drank a thousand bottles together. We dug and buried a hundred chests on as many islands and sailed the seven seas in search of many more. All for nothin'.

A werewolf! I seen a lot o' things in me time but I ain't never 'eard o' nothin' so sinister as that. This place must be cursed.' A single tear ran from the corner of one lonely eye.

'It's cursed all right,' said Stanley, handing him a handkerchief.

'Well, blisterin' coconuts, if ever a piece o' news knocked the wind out o' me sails it's this.'

'What is your name?' asked Mrs Carelli.

'MacDowell, ma'am. I already told yer!'

'No, I mean your first name.'

'MacDowell.'

'So what is your last name?'

'MacDowell.'

'So your full name is MacDowell MacDowell?'

'No ma'am, just MacDowell, though some folks call me Dead-Eye MacDowell. Yer know, owing to the patch. Lost me left goggle in a fight, I did. Very painful.'

'That must have been some mean old buccaneer you fought that took out an eye,' said Mrs Carelli.

'Weren't no buccaneer, ma'am. T'was a bear!'

'A bear?' they all cried out at once.

'Aye, lad,' said MacDowell, turning to Stanley and looking close with one eye. 'Seven feet tall and hairy as a mammoth. Didn't like me diggin' a hole near his patch in the woods and clawed me badly. It was yer Great-Uncle Bart that saved me that time. Blasted it to the other side o' the woods with his old musket.'

Stanley sat with his mouth open and wide eyes staring. And as they listened to all the old tales of MacDowell and Swift it grew late into the night and the fire was on its last legs.

Mr and Mrs Carelli sat snoozing in their chairs, but old MacDowell was still going strong with a bottle of whisky clutched in his hand and a tall tale reeling away. Stanley listened in fascination and wonder, but he felt his eyelids dropping.

'Perhaps I should show you to your room now, sir,' he murmured.

'Aye, lad. That'd be just fine. I'm in need of a good kip. Thank yer very much.'

Stanley led him upstairs and MacDowell closed the door on his host, bidding him goodnight. When he had sat a moment on the bed and taken a good look at his room, he looked into the mirror on the wash cabinet. He scratched at his whiskery chin and fell on to the bed in a fit of whisky-fuelled snoring.

Retrieving the map

An ancient silver casket sat in damp darkness.
No chink of daylight was around to shine
upon its delicately crafted surface, or pick out
the colours that came upon it in the sun.

Until now.

Stanley Buggles' grubby hands reached in
and held the silver casket around its belly,
retrieving it for one short moment. A

moment that was long enough to take out the ancient map that lay inside.

This was the very map that he and Daisy had discovered was a plan of the island they were on. Crampton Rock!

Daisy Grouse was Stanley's closest friend. The niece of the lighthouse keeper, she lived a stone's throw from Stanley when she was visiting her uncle,

which seemed to be most of the time.
Together they had seen off the worst of
pirate life, and right now they had business to
attend to.

The old map that lay in their possession
had an 'X marks the spot' that was aching
to be discovered. They had found the
whereabouts of the cross on the map.
But frustratingly, its centre lay in the

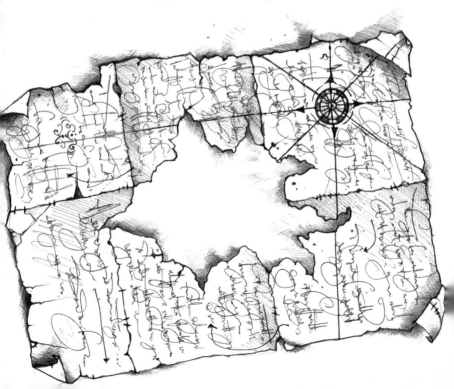

Darkling house, down in the village.

They had checked and double-checked, but each time they came back to the very same spot: the spooky, ramshackle old hut that Edmund Darkling had made his family home.

'Daisy, I've made a decision,' announced Stanley.

Daisy looked at him expectantly.

'Well then …!' she prompted. 'What is it? Are you going to cut your hair?' She laughed.

He ignored her sense of humour. 'We have to get into the cellar of the old Darkling place. We can go during the day because the Darklings sleep for most of it, we know that. As long as we aren't seen by the villagers, we can have a snoop around.'

'Stanley, we've been in enough trouble lately,' Daisy pointed out.

'I know, but this whole treasure-seeking thing will grind to a halt unless we can get inside there. It must be under the floor,' he persisted.

Daisy had to concede the point. Unless they found their way into the house, they would never get any further!

'Don't think of it as breaking into the house, Daisy. Think of it as taking a short cut to where we're going,' Stanley chirped, a big smile on his face.

'Oh, yes. Very good, Stanley. I'll tell that to the court!' Daisy quipped.

They set off into the village, map in hand, arguing as they went.

Stanley reflected briefly on his previous actions. He had been forced to break into the Darkling home to retrieve vital evidence, something that had landed him in serious trouble. He knew that his good intentions caused him to go astray at times, and that he must be careful not to get too carried away.

And as they walked, a curtain twitched in a nearby window and an eye appeared through the netting. It watched them as they went and observed until they were out of sight.

Seeking an Ally

Daisy looked around, scouting for anyone who might be watching them. If anyone had done so, they would have seen Stanley's feet disappearing through the fuel-store entrance as he slid headlong into the basement of the Darkling home. And then they would have seen Daisy follow, pulling the door closed on its loose hinges.

But no one did.

The entrance to the cellar through the fuel store was at the back of the house and it was out of view from the steady flow of people in the village.

Inside, the warmth of the sun disappeared and was replaced by a musty, damp cold with only shafts of light to point the way. The floor was empty and the walls were scattered with poorly mounted shelving, home to bits of this and that.

'Nothing in here, Stanley,' whispered Daisy.

'It's below ground that matters, Daisy. That map is old, very old. Older than this building, for sure. What's here, if anything, is below us!' answered Stanley, forgetting where he was and raising his voice in excitement.

'Shhh!' urged Daisy. 'They'll hear us!'

They felt at the floor. It was wet and hard, with huge stone slabs laid from wall to wall. Too heavy, thought Stanley, for either him or Daisy, or for that matter, both of them together.

A click, click, clicking sound came from above.

And then a sniff, sniff, sniff. Then more clicking. Movement of some kind. They both froze, then Daisy realized what it was.

'It's the dog,' she breathed, wringing her hands. 'It's Steadman, the Darkling dog.'

And no sooner had she said it than Steadman began to bark. Louder and louder and furiously leaping about in the room above, until the whole house was awake.

But luckily his noise disguised Stanley and Daisy's scrambling as they wheedled their way back outside into daylight, scurrying away like little beetles from under a stone.

They headed into the open warmth of the village and tried to mingle with the crowd.

But they had been seen. Young Berkeley, one of the Darkling twins, had observed that they were up to no good.

*

As far as the treasure seekers were concerned, they had not been spotted. They headed back to the Hall and unfolded more plans.

'We can't move those slabs, Daisy. But I have an idea. We can break them up.'

'Oh great, Stanley. Another good idea. You're not going to stop at breaking and entering. You're going to smash the place up now. And I guess you'll be doing that without making any noise, will you?' she asked, with her arms held aloft. 'We need help,' she insisted. 'But who in their right mind would join us in a treasure hunt through someone else's basement? We need someone trustworthy but with a hint of mischief about them, and a glint of piracy in their eye. Ah, if only Admiral Swift was still here!' she sighed.

Stanley's expression changed from a glum, forlorn sulk into a wide-eyed, villainous grin.

'Daisy, you're a genius. Well done!' he laughed. He kissed her on the cheek and began dancing in twirls along the cobbles until he was so dizzy he fell flat on his face.

'What's the matter with you?' Daisy asked, wiping the wet from her face.

'You need to come and meet someone,' insisted Stanley, nursing a bashed elbow. He grabbed her by the wrist and pulled her along at a pace.

When they reached the Hall, MacDowell was lying out in the sun with his huge hat pulled over his face.

Daisy stared at the long loose shape in front of her. She had never seen such a gnarled old weasel in all her time on the Rock. His hat was wider than his shoulders and his holey tights were wrapped around the most ridiculous pair of legs she had ever seen.

His huge buckled shoes pointed up to the sun and revealed a hole in each sole.

'Meet MacDowell,' said Stanley.

'A dear old friend of Admiral Swift's.'

'Oh … erm, pleased to meet you, sir,' said Daisy, performing a limp handshake

with MacDowell's craggy, dried-up palm. As his hand closed around hers, Daisy realized that his frail figure belied his real strength.

'Well, tickle me timbers,' MacDowell started. 'If ever I saw a pretty little face well there it is, right in front o' me. Pleased to meet yer, Miss Daisy.'

Daisy rolled her eyes at Stanley. She hated nothing more than someone telling her she was pretty.

Stanley was eager to know more about MacDowell and his adventures with Admiral Swift, before he and Daisy unfolded their plan.

MacDowell had no idea, but he was about to be interviewed for the best job on Crampton Rock.

'Tell me more about how you met my great-uncle,' said Stanley.

'Well, Stanley,' MacDowell began, 'I am an inventor by trade. A poor one, yes, I admit. But that doesn't stop me from makin' the effort. At one time I travelled the seas in an old fishing boat, selling my wares at every port I could find and scratchin' a meagre living. I came across your great-uncle when he was down on his luck, fresh out o' the navy, injured and without a penny to his name. I had found myself in the same destitute position and it wouldn't have started if we 'adn't been desperate.'

'What wouldn't have happened?' asked Stanley.

'Oh, the pirate thing. It were unintentional. We watched a boat leaving shore and we'd noticed a few well-to-do types climbing aboard. Yer know, fancy folk wi' money in their pockets and gold about their necks.

'I had agreed to give yer Great-Uncle Bart a lift on me boat and we got caught in a storm. In the thick of it, another boat came into view.'

'The rich people's boat,' predicted Daisy.

'Aye, lass, the very same,' MacDowell replied with a sigh. 'We helped their boat through the worst of it, but we claimed everything they had in return. It was a dreadful business, Stanley. It should not have happened, but it did. And it carried on.'

'You're not a man to be trusted then?' suggested Stanley.

'I wasn't then,' he admitted, giving another, deeper, sigh. 'And neither was yer old great-uncle. But those days are behind me now. I only wish me old mate was 'ere to enjoy the quiet life with.' He finished speaking, closed his eyes and soaked up the sun.

Stanley stepped aside to whisper to Daisy. He had decided he liked MacDowell. There was something brutally honest about him: he wasn't trying to hide his past and there wasn't an ounce of threat to him.

'He's just a whisky-guzzling old buccaneer who's grown tired of the sea and his pirate ways, much as Great-Uncle Bart did,' Stanley explained to Daisy.

'Mmmm, I'm not sure. I don't see why we should trust him. He looks like a villain, and he's as sly as an old fox.'

Stanley was not always such a great listener. If he listened to anyone, it was Daisy, but he had an awful habit of ignoring what he didn't want to hear.

He decided that Daisy had made a
decision based on how MacDowell looked,
and that annoyed him. But he'd keep the
peace for now.

Just deserts

The following afternoon, Stanley found out that he and old MacDowell had something in common: they both had the ability to sleep for most of the day. They bumped into each other at breakfast, which, as Mrs Carelli rightly pointed out, was not normally at three o'clock of an afternoon.

They sat together at the kitchen table,

locked in conversation and getting on furiously.
MacDowell was intrigued by Crampton Rock,
and full of questions for Stanley.

'Tell me one thing, lad. Somethin' is troublin'
me,' began MacDowell.

'Fire away,' said Stanley.

'Well, whenever I looks around me outside,
the streets is full and the folks is goin' about
their business, and I see a dog now and then.
Not the same dog, mind you. Lots o' dogs. Big
dogs, little dogs, hairy dogs, skinny dogs,
chubby little fat dogs ...'

Stanley knew what was coming.

'Now, it's come to me attention that they all
'ave a little something in common!'

MacDowell paused and looked at Stanley,
his eyes a little wider and his face a little
closer.

'Carry on,' said Stanley, smiling.

'Three legs, Stanley. They all got three legs,' he exclaimed.

'It's the wolf,' announced Stanley. 'The werewolf! I did warn you that this place is cursed. There isn't a dog on the island that has escaped an attack from that thing without losing a limb.'

MacDowell stared at Stanley in disbelief.

'Well, sufferin' seagulls, I don't believe it. If ever a place was cursed it's this one! Are yer sure there ain't no wolf at present, Stanley? I'd hate to lose a branch from me tree, so to speak.'

'A branch from your …? Oh, I see what you mean,' said Stanley. 'Erm, no … there is no wolf right now.

We hope it will not return.'

'Good news, lad,' answered MacDowell.
'For an old man who's taking it easy, that's
good news.'

'Actually,' began Stanley rather gingerly,
'I had rather hoped I might enlist your help!'

'Oh?'

'Well, you see, I have this map. An old
map.'

But he was stopped in his tracks.

'Oh Stanley, please. Stop. Don't tell me yer
taking me on a treasure
hunt. I've 'ad enough
o' treasure huntin' to
last me a lifetime.
I've seen more maps
than I've had hot
dinners. It's always the
same: a load o' work,

only to find that someone else got there before you did. It's 'appened to me a thousand times and the last time I made the effort and came out of it penniless, I swore I'd never let it happen again.

'And besides,' MacDowell continued, 'I got one o' me little inventions boilin' away in me brain. Once I gets an idea, that's it, I can't stop. Now, do yer think there's somewhere I can use a little workspace?'

And Stanley realized that his companion was nothing more than a retired old sea dog with all the 'pirate' already knocked out of his sails. He gave a big sigh and went to tell Daisy what was, for her, the good news.

As Stanley was returning from his visit to Daisy in the lighthouse, he noticed a commotion down in the village. He wandered closer to the crowd of people outside the courthouse.

'It's Mister Darkling, Stanley,' muttered a man who Stanley recognized as one of the fishermen who also helped out in the court. 'He's been sentenced to imprisonment for the attempt he made on your life. He's got what he deserves.'

Stanley walked a little nearer. The crowd was jostling and shoving, and cries of 'Murderer!' went up in the air. Mrs Darkling and her children, Annabelle, Berkeley and Olive, were being escorted safely home through the swarm, and Mr Darkling jeered back at the onlookers as he was taken away to prison.

Stanley did not feel particularly happy at this outcome. He didn't feel that the Darklings were a threat to him any more.

Yes, when they had come to the Hall and tried to claim it as their own, it had been a terrible time for him. But they were a family, with three children – and yes, they were a little odd, to say the least, but nonetheless they would be better off together.

That was the reason that Stanley had given when he refused to give evidence in the trial. But the strange laws of Crampton Rock meant that the trial continued without him, and now the Darkling family faced a lifetime of only seeing their husband and father through a barred window.

Stanley's heart sank. He felt almost guilty, even though he could have died by the dirty deeds of Edmund Darkling.

He wandered back up the cobbled climb to the Hall, and as he reached the door MacDowell and Victor were leaving the house with their arms full.

'Good news, lad. Victor 'as given me permission to use 'is workspace down at the candle shop. 'E says he won't be needin' it yet, not until he gets the business back up and running,' chirped MacDowell. 'Mrs Carelli says that if it's all right with you, I can stay a while and try and make meself a bit o' money before I move on,' he explained. 'What do yer say, Stanley?'

'Er … yes, fine, Mac. It's fine.'

'Ah, Stanley, you're pure gold. From the tip o' yer nose to the ends o' yer toes, you're pure gold. Wait till yer see me invention. I'll be made o' money before yer can say *crab soup*.'

Stanley scratched his head. He'd heard that expression before somewhere.

He stood and watched MacDowell and Victor head into the village, then turned inside to tell Mrs Carelli the Darkling news.

As the evening drew in, the warm aroma of home-cooked food filled the kitchen, and as the light was dropping Victor and MacDowell returned. Victor had a look of amusement on his face and MacDowell was looking pleased with himself.

'Ah, Stanley. If ever there was a man to make a sensible judgement, it'd be you.'

Stanley, sitting in his favourite chair, eyed old MacDowell quizzically.

'What would yer be guessin' this was then?' MacDowell asked, revealing something that he had concealed inside his long coat.

Stanley stared at the contraption.
'Erm … it looks like a wheel on a
stick.'

'Aha. Wrong!' insisted
MacDowell. 'This, Stanley,
is the Crampton Canine
Lost Limb Support
thingy. And
tomorrow,' he
continued, 'there will be many a piece o'
silver crossing the palm of old MacDowell
down in the village square. Thank you, thank
you, ladies and gentlemen.' He took a bow as
Victor and Mrs Carelli clapped and Stanley
stared in disbelief.

'Are you serious?' asked Stanley. 'You're
going to sell those to the dog owners in
the village?'

'Aye, lad. If ever there was a plan to make

money on the Rock, this be it.' He was clearly as pleased as Punch with his idea.

That night, as Stanley pulled his covers over him, he wondered if there would ever be a way forward with the map. Would he ever get any further than the damp darkness of the Darkling cellar?

Down the corridor, old MacDowell was drinking himself to sleep with a bottle of grog that he kept tucked under his pillow, dreaming of the riches that he hoped were coming his way.

And down in the cold, harsh darkness of Crampton jailhouse, Edmund Darkling listened to the lock turning in the door as he settled into his cell.

A clear night was framed by his barred window.

There has to be a way out, he thought. No man can live like this, certainly not for long.

Perhaps he would have to resort to desperate measures: measures that would ensure his escape but would be a terrible burden for the people of Crampton Rock.

The next time Stanley and Daisy saw old MacDowell, he was down on his luck already, sitting on the harbour wall with his head in his hands.

'Ahoy there, MacDowell!' cheered Stanley.

'Ahoy yerself,' he said glumly.

'What's wrong, Mac?' started Stanley. 'You were full of the joys of spring yesterday.'

'Well, to cut a long story short, I made me first sale and an hour later I 'ad to give me silver back and scrap all me money-makin' plans.'

'Why?' the two asked together.

'Well, a little old lady from the village bought the *wheel on a stick*, as you called it. She attached it to the dog, where its front leg used to be, an' it all seemed to work fine,' MacDowell explained.

'And?' urged Daisy.

'And then it ran down to the harbour and couldn't stop when it arrived.'

'Oh!' said Stanley.

'Yes, oh indeed! Now, did yer say yer had a map that wanted lookin' at?'

Stanley grinned at Daisy. At last, they had the help they needed.

The Greatest Secret

Despite Stanley's dislike of Edmund Darkling's imprisonment, it meant that his plan would turn out perfectly. It became noticeable that Grace Darkling and the children had taken to visiting Mr Darkling at dusk, when the streets had emptied and the light was low.

Ideal circumstances for treasure seekers.

MacDowell had been fully briefed by

Daisy and Stanley as he gazed over the map.

'Well shiver me timbers, 'ow on earth did yer work this one out? Are yer sure yer right?' he questioned.

'As sure as sure can be,' claimed Daisy.

These were the terms under which MacDowell was entrusted into the alliance:

They weren't to be seen entering through the fuel store at any cost.

When they were inside, they weren't to excite the dog in the house above them.

And most importantly, MacDowell would be paid by Stanley and Daisy for his efforts, depending on what they ended up with.

'Well it all sounds fine and dandy to me, young buccaneers,' he giggled. 'I'm not so keen on the sound o' the Darkling place, but I guess I'll learn to live wi' that one.'

The Smugglers' Secret

When darkness had dusted its way among the streets and buildings of the Rock, the treasure-seekers alliance gathered under the dim lamplight of the square and headed across the village. Under the pretence that they were helping MacDowell on his project, they headed to Victor's workshop, where they had a clear view of the Darkling place.

They sat in candlelight for some time, and eventually saw the prison visitors heading for the jailhouse.

Three shapes left the huddled cosiness of Victor's shop, and ventured into the cold of an early evening. The bandy legs of MacDowell slithered down the chute, and Stanley and Daisy followed.

MacDowell sparked up a flame and held a lighted piece of paper aloft. Stanley held out a candle and a yellow warmth filled the dank space.

Pulling out a long crowbar from inside his coat, MacDowell jemmied up a huge stone flag. With help from his aides, MacDowell levered this way and that, lifting each flag-stone in turn.

'Nothing so far, Stanley!' he gasped. He blew into the air with hot breaths for a moment, sweat pouring from his brow.

'What about over there?' suggested Stanley, pointing to an as yet undisturbed corner.

And as the slab in the far corner was raised, the reason for the wet floor became clear. There, underneath the last stone, was a well, cut into the rock below. Water came up to the brim, and Daisy dipped her hand in. She lifted it to her mouth and smelled it.

'Salt water,' she said.

MacDowell got down on his knees and tasted, just to be sure.

Stanley held the candle over it, but he could see nothing.

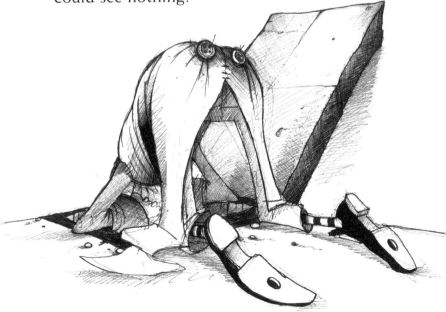

'What now?' he asked.

'We wait, Stanley,' suggested MacDowell.

'What for?'

'Come on, Stanley, use your noggin. It's salt water!' Daisy exclaimed. 'From the sea! When the tide's out, we can climb in!'

'Ahhhhh! GREAT!' beamed Stanley. 'When's next tide out?'

'Tomorrow afternoon,' announced Daisy.

'Then, me dears, we shall return!' cried MacDowell, who seemed revived with thoughts of treasure. He heaved the last stone back into position, but, just as they were ready to leave, a door slammed above them.

A moment of panic ensued. The trio were scared into stillness as they listened to what they were sure must be the return of the Darklings. MacDowell held up the flats of his hands, gesturing to them not to move.

Stanley blew out his candle.

Voices carried above. 'What's wrong with Steadman?' they heard Berkeley ask. The black dog was sniffing and growling at the floor. 'What is it, boy?' he persisted.

The dog was clearly disturbed by the activity in the basement. He whimpered and scratched at the bare boards.

'Berkeley, take a look down there, would you? Something has upset him.' It was Grace, clearly distressed at leaving her husband at the jailhouse. The three conspirators could hear the girls following her upstairs.

Berkeley opened the hatch from the kitchen and climbed into the space below. It was pure black, and he held a lamp to find his way. Steadman stood at the top of the steps, barking, with his head poking through the opening.

The treasure seekers were piled into one
corner, their backs turned to Berkeley. He
held the lamp towards them. Under the light
of the lamp was what looked to Berkeley like
an old sheet hung on the
wall. But unbeknown
to him, it was
the back of
MacDowell's
coat. Inside it,
Daisy and
Stanley were
tucked neatly
on either side of
their scrawny
companion, their eyes shut tight and their
bodies clenched in fear of discovery.

Berkeley backed away. He tripped.
Something was there. Something on the floor

behind him. It was MacDowell's crowbar, still lying on the stone flags.

'Are you all right, Berkeley?' came a voice. It was Olive, his twin sister.

'Fine,' he called.

'Come on,' she said. 'Mother wants you upstairs!'

And to the great relief of the hiding trio, he disappeared back up the wooden staircase.

The three companions scrambled up the chute and stole out into the night, knowing full well that in only a short time, they would need to return.

The hours dragged. When they arose the following morning, the sun was cascading across the harbour, but Stanley was eager for the day to hurry along. Both he and Daisy had big hopes for what might lie beneath the Rock.

'A great hoard of treasure has placed its picture in my mind,' announced Stanley, 'with twinkling diamonds and dazzling, jewelled shapes of gold.'

'I hope you're right,' said Daisy. 'After all this trouble, you deserve it.' But Daisy had more sense. 'Just a modest trunk of pirate gold is all I expect,' she laughed. 'Nothing more. Just enough to pay me a handsome living and leave me in comfort for the rest of my life, that's all. Oh, and a handful of coins for the slab-lifter,' she joked.

The two of them were sitting on the harbour wall. Stanley had been whiling away the hours looking for crabs. He had a line of shells and bits of bone all laid out neatly in front of him.

MacDowell shuffled up alongside them.

'That's a smart-lookin' assortment o' beach

life if ever I saw one. This is a funny old place though, Stanley. Are yer sure yer not breaking some ancient law of the Rock by takin' them there shells and bones.'

'Not as far as I know,' laughed Stanley. 'Shells are shells. They don't belong to anyone in particular, just to whoever picks them up and takes them, I guess.'

They sat in the sun for a little longer and watched the tide move slowly back. When they were absolutely sure that it was far enough out, they made their move, splitting up and reassembling at the bottom of the village.

Something Wickedly Weird

MacDowell was the look-out this time, bundling the other two unceremoniously down the chute. And then he followed, sailing down into the damp darkness and not caring that his shabby clothes would now be soaking wet.

But someone was watching, still and silent, taking it all in, squinting his eyes at the faces and making sure that who he saw was who he thought he knew.

All the while, the treasure seekers made their every move without speaking a single word. Each was fully aware that should they speak and disturb the house, they would jeopardize everything.

After all, they were about to uncover the greatest secret that Crampton Rock had ever kept.

MacDowell fished around in the half-dark. He had left his crowbar by mistake the previous night, and finally found it propped up against the wall. He was certain he hadn't left it there, but he grabbed hold of it and began to lever up the stone flag in the corner.

Sure enough, by the light of Stanley's candle the deep void of the well could be seen. Yes, it was dark and damp, but it led somewhere. A flight of steps led down through the narrow opening.

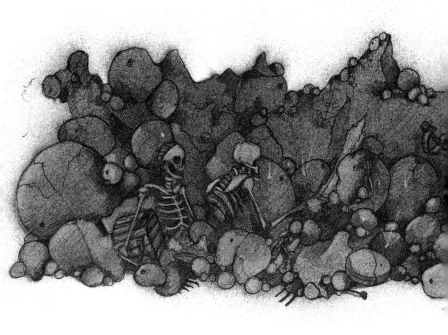

'After you then, Stanley, Daisy,' said
MacDowell. Then he followed them into
the void, leaving the basement in emptiness
until they returned.

Or so they thought. But in the corner,
where they themselves had hidden from
Berkeley the previous night, two moon-like
eyes shone in the darkness. And when the
treasure seekers had disappeared into the

uncertainty of the black hole, a small figure
stepped out into the open and poked its
inquisitive head down the well.

Deep down and further in, the three treasure
seekers squinted into the darkness ahead.
Daisy stood beside Stanley, eyeing the rough
wall of the hollow. She moved closer, shoving
past him.

'Stanley, bring your candle up to the wall,' she said. She placed her hand against the coarse surface. As the light came nearer, the rock face twinkled in the dark.

Three faces leered up close and gasped in astonishment. Stanley raked the candle along the wall, and it was the same as far as they could see: small splinters of gold embedded into the rock. On and on and on. And old, fragmented skeletons of desperate pirates, open-mouthed skulls, bones clutching tightly to chests of rotting wood. Some had blades tucked inside their ribs, and others had severed limbs. There was no doubt that many a battle had been fought on the Rock.

They looked ahead to where the passage grew narrow again.

As they walked on, it tailed off into more little tunnels. On they went, this way, that

way, upwards, downwards, sideways. Long
honeycombed networks of passageways all
littered with jewelled stones for as far as they
could see.

The three buccaneers were speechless.
Save for a few gasps of wonderment, they
barely managed to speak to one another.

'Wallopin' weevils! I ain't never laid eyes on
such a treat in all me days. The devil sure was
full of 'imself the day he put this place
together. It's enough to turn any sane man
into the worst of sea dogs.'

Stanley didn't have a clue what
MacDowell was saying.

'This ain't no ordinary find, Stanley. Yer
need to keep this one firmly under yer hat.
There's serious consequences in this gettin'
out in the open.'

'What do you mean by that?' Daisy asked.

'Listen now,' he began, 'and listen good. This ain't no buried treasure we're lookin' at. Oh no, this is a gold mine. A place where gold occurs naturally in the rock. Where it's dug from in the first place. Are yer with me?'

'Aye, captain,' said Stanley. 'I'm with you.'

'Daisy?'

'Aye, aye, sir. I get what you're saying.'

'If this 'ere secret creeps outside o' this old mine, you can kiss goodbye to Candlestick Hall and every other thing in sight. If ever yer needed to keep a secret, me dears, this'll be it.'

'I'm not sure what you're saying,' quizzed Daisy as she squinted through the darkness.

'Well pin yer ears back now and take heed. If the rest o' the pirate world gets to know that Crampton Rock is hiding a gold mine, they'll be here in a flash. Them and every gold prospector that ever lived, chinking away at these hollows until every last little piece has been claimed. And when that's been done, this whole island will collapse under the strain and you'd better find another Rock to put down your roots in.'

Stanley stared at Daisy and she stared back at him. Their wide grins had turned into serious expressions at the thought of what might come.

They turned back and tiptoed out through the mine, back out into the cellar, replacing the stone flag in its place … where just ahead of them, someone sneaked away unseen.

Desperate
measures

Edmund Darkling awoke in his cell. The
same four walls were still around him. He had
only been here for a short space of time, but
frustration and desperation had already taken
their toll. He was not prepared to give in to
this dreadful life of half-existence when he
knew there was a way out.

That night Grace Darkling came to visit,

with the children following at her heels. She was allowed a short while to sit with her husband, but before the conversation had even begun they were usually herded back out into the street.

'Grace, I am at my wits' end,' declared Mr Darkling. 'I need to walk outside under the moonlight. I need to feel the earth beneath my feet. My children will grow up outside these walls and I will be confined inside them. I'm sorry, Grace, but I must make my escape in the only way I know how.'

'No, Edmund, please. Wait. There is another way, I'm sure. We can make a plea to the court. They may show some leniency if we wait a while,' Grace begged.

'There is no other way. Prepare yourself; you will not see me in here again after tonight.'

Moments later, Mrs Darkling was dragged
in tears to the door of the jailhouse. She stole
through the village under the moonlight,
with the children
trailing behind
her.

Stanley was tucked up in his bed, trying to
drop off to sleep. The image of the gold mine
had stayed with him all afternoon, and he
could barely contain his excitement. But he
knew MacDowell was right, it was a secret
that must never escape. It would put the Rock

at risk, and the cost would be too great.

Each of the treasure seekers had made a promise: that they would never, as long as they lived, take a single piece of gold from beneath the surface of Crampton Rock.

The slab of stone was put back in place, and the secret was safe again.

But Stanley worried that this great secret would wheedle its way out. And if it did, it would be his fault. He climbed out of bed and walked to the window, rubbing his eyes. He could see the brim of the ocean lapping up against the harbour. The tide was in and he knew that no one could get into the mines right now.

And he knew that every time he looked out to sea he would think of the mines, with their long honeycombed trails lying beneath Crampton Rock like a huge beehive.

Whenever the tide was out he would feel nervous. Nervous that the bare sand, as it dried to a burning hot surface in the sun, was the sign of an open door down into the twinkling void.

And what if someone found their way in? There must be at least one way in from the cliffs, thought Stanley. Sure, it might not be big enough for someone to creep through, but nonetheless it preyed on his mind. 'Arrrrrrrghhhhhhh-hooooooooooooowwwl,' came an unearthly cry through the air as Stanley stared into the darkness.

His heart thundered. He had heard that cry before. But surely he hadn't heard what he thought he had heard.

'Aaaooooooooooooooooooooooo,' it came again. Only this time clearer, almost as if the howler was getting stronger and finding his voice.

It rang through the night and spots of light appeared in a few of the houses as candles were lit and curtains pulled back.

And then Stanley was sure, absolutely sure, that he saw something long and black and slender sleeking through the village.

He rubbed his eyes again. 'I'm dreaming,' he murmured, and climbed back into bed.

But as he slept the noise continued, and he dreamed of the wolf's return. He was following the great beast, pursuing it through the smugglers' mines, pushing through the long dark tunnels and thundering over the rocks and stones. But he was too late. The wolf had got there first, and taken hold of someone or something. A great moan echoed out across the Rock.

Stanley woke with a start. Silence reigned. The night was still.

In the end he must have drifted back to sleep, but it felt to Stanley like he'd been up all night.

A loud knock at the door disturbed him. He looked at the old clock by his bedside and saw that it was early. Mrs Carelli was calling to him.

'Stanley! Stanley! Can you come down, lad,' she cried in a soft voice. He knew something was wrong. He leaped up and jumped quickly into his clothes, blustering down the stairs.

His good friend Bartley and the old lady Greta were there, from the gypsy camp out on the moor.

'Sit down, Stanley,' instructed Mrs Carelli. But he stayed standing and stared at their serious expressions.

No one smiled or exchanged pleasantries.

It was too early for a social call and that meant only one thing.

Bad news!

'What is it?' Stanley asked.

'It's my brother Phinn,' Bartley began. 'Something took him in the night, lad. Something beastly. It looks like the curse of the werewolf has returned to the island.'

Stanley felt sick. He asked them to tell him once more, so that he could be sure he heard them, though there was nothing else on earth that could have sounded worse to his ears.

A wave of dizziness came over him and Mrs Carelli gently took his shoulders and put him in a chair.

'No!' cried Stanley. 'Not Phinn. Are you sure?' And then the previous night came flooding back to him. The strange howl, the lights in the windows, the black shape slinking through the village. He'd been right. He really *had* seen it.

'Phinn was returning from the inn alone,' explained Bartley. 'We had taken a drink together, and returned separately. Not for any real reason – I was talking with some of the fishermen and agreed to catch up with him on the moor. But when I did, it was too late.'

Bartley dropped his head and hid the tears that were rolling down his cheeks.

Only a stone's throw from where they sat in tears remembering their good friend Phinn, a commotion was bubbling in the jailhouse. The prison warder was inspecting the cells.

Mostly they
were empty,
save for the
odd short-term
visitor. But at
the far end
lay the cell where Edmund Darkling had
been condemned to spend the rest of his
days.

The warder turned the long key in the
lock, pushed down the handle and opened
the door – then looked on in astonishment as
he saw that the cell was empty.

The bars
of the window had
somehow been twisted
and broken to force an opening.
And in the far corner of the room, a pair of
shoes and a pile of torn and tattered clothing
were the only signs that Edmund Darkling
had ever even been there.

7

Complications

In the days that followed, things began to change dramatically on the island. The look-outs returned to their watchtowers at dusk, which was a sure sign that the villagers believed the wolf had returned. Stanley watched from his window and with a growing sense of worry he saw the silhouettes of figures clambering up the stilts to the very top.

A sense of fear and darkness returned to the Rock and on top of this, Stanley and Daisy were greatly saddened at the loss of their good friend Phinn. His lonesome grave now stood out on the bleak moor, with only the wild winds to keep it company.

And to worsen matters further, the gypsies had decided they had no choice but to leave the island again.

They knew that one day they would return
to the peaceful charm of the Rock, but right
now the same dreadful creature that had
driven them away before had worked its
wicked way once again.

Stanley and Daisy stood at the harbour
with the Carellis and a handful of villagers as
they watched the wooden wagons crawl
down across the moor. The long timber trail
snaked through the hills and finally arrived
on the cobbles, making their way to the ferry.

One wagon stopped and out came Bartley. His huge figure stooped to climb out through the small frame of the door. His eyes were reddened and he threw his bulk around Daisy and then Stanley.

'Before we go, Stanley, I thought you might like to take this,' he said, struggling to get the words out through his tears, and he put something into Stanley's hands. It was Phinn's hat.

'He always said it brought him luck,' he

continued. 'It's just a shame he wasn't wearing it the night he was attacked.'

Stanley and Daisy begged him and Greta to stay. They could leave the wagons out on the moor and stay at the Hall. Sure, it would be chaos, but it was big enough for all of them.

But no, the decision had been made *for* them. That was how they saw it.

'One day, Stanley, we will return. And you had better promise me that when we do, you will still be here,' said Bartley, shaking his hand and almost crushing it without even realizing.

'I shall be here,' said Stanley, brushing off a tear and massaging his fingers. 'I'll be waiting for you.'

They stood at the harbour wall until the ferry had grown tiny and the waving hands had mingled with the flapping wings of the seagulls that followed them.

As they returned to the Hall, someone from the Mayoress's office was nailing posters to every post he could find.

Stanley and Daisy stopped and stared. Surely not!

Edmund Darkling escaped from his prison cell!

'How on earth could he possibly manage that? Those bars are made of the strongest iron,' claimed Stanley.

And then he began to wonder.

'What is it?' quizzed Daisy.

'Oh, erm … nothing. I had a thought, but I'm sure it's wrong,' he mumbled.

'Well come on then,' she said as they stood staring at the poster. 'Don't keep me in the dark, Stanley. What *is* your little thought?'

'Well, when the Darklings first came to claim the Hall, Greta explained something to us about their past. Do you remember?'

'You mean, about their connection to the werewolf, that they had an ancestor who had suffered the curse?'

'Exactly.' Stanley grimaced. 'A direct blood-line to the wolf, the very man who built Candlestick Hall in the first place. Brice Darkling. Bitten by the wolf, but lived to tell the tale and father a line of children who spread the lupine strains through generations.'

'Are you saying that *Edmund Darkling* is our werewolf?' Daisy asked, open-mouthed.

'Maybe.' Stanley was unsure. 'I know it sounds ridiculous, but how else could he break through those bars?'

Their discussion was broken in two.

'Blisterin' blood boils, whatever next? Escaped criminals! Werewolves! Folks leavin' the island in despair! This place be goin' downhill, lad.'

It was MacDowell, scratching his head and staring at the poster over their shoulders.

They chatted away, wandering into the village, and found themselves outside the candle shop. The door was slightly open, and inside Victor was working away.

The three of them went in to say hello and sat a while, talking over the unfolding drama and predicting what would become of the days ahead.

But Daisy could see the old Darkling place from where she sat, and she caught sight of something she didn't like. She nudged Stanley and they stared out through the window.

Young Berkeley was heading around to the back of the house, and they could hear the hatch of the fuel store lifting and a small person disappearing down the chute. Berkeley's sisters were in the kitchen, but little did they know what he was up to under their very feet.

MacDowell had caught on, and now he too was filled with panic. What was the boy up to? How much did he know? And when would they get the chance to find out what he was doing in the Darkling cellar?

The Littlest Pirate

It was late the following afternoon when they spotted Berkeley again. Daisy had been out fishing with her uncle in the morning, and when they returned with their catch she took a good amount of fish up to the Hall for Mrs Carelli. She stayed a while and they all sat out in the sun, basking on the lawn.

They watched the sea move back into
the distance and Stanley wondered about
the mine being exposed while the tide
was out.

Then Berkeley ran across the harbour. He
was on his own, and most likely up to no
good. Stanley got to his feet, watching
Berkeley's every move. But he'd gone right
down into the village and was now out of
sight.

'Anybody fancy a walk?' asked Stanley.

Right away, the rest of the treasure-seekers
alliance were on their feet, trotting along in
the sun in order to spy on the young lad.

Stanley had been given a key of his own
for the shop, and this made things a little
easier when they were snooping. They cut
across the back of the shops and houses and
entered Victor's place through the rear door,

piling up at the window, shoving their faces at the little square panes and forcing their eyelids wider in the hope that they would see more.

They knocked a row of candles to the floor as they pushed up to the window, each one breaking in half as it landed, before rolling across the floor.

And again, from where they watched, they could see a small figure disappearing around the back of the house. They listened quietly. Bang! That small noise told them that the fuel-store door had just been opened and closed.

'Why doesn't he just go through the house from the kitchen?' quizzed Daisy.

'He's like us,' said Stanley. 'He doesn't want to be discovered. His mother knows only too well what a pest he is, always up to no good.'

'Very true,' said Daisy.

Back outside they went, looking this way and that.

Luckily the warm afternoon had sent most people down on to the baking sand, and the village was deserted.

They couldn't decide how to enter the basement. They needed a silent approach so that they could stealthily look in on mischievous Berkeley, but there was no way of sneaking in because the drop was too dramatic – they always landed with a thud and went rolling across the floor. There wasn't really any other way.

Or was there?

'I got it, lad,' claimed MacDowell and he explained some hare-brained plan to Stanley that Daisy wasn't sure about at all. She watched in great doubt as MacDowell clasped tightly on to Stanley's ankles and let the rest of him dangle down the chute so that he could peer in.

If Stanley kicked his right foot, it meant that he wanted lowering further in. And his left? That meant there was danger and he needed pulling back. Who knew what dark danger might be lurking there? Perhaps if they were right about Edmund he was hiding out in there, and Berkeley was bringing him food and water.

If ever Stanley had needed to trust MacDowell, it was now.

But Stanley could see and hear nothing. No sights or sounds that gave anything away.

Lower he went, further and further ... until old MacDowell's back could take no more.

'Ahh, Stanley, old MacDowell don't 'ave the strength 'e used to 'ave!' he cried, letting go of Stanley's ankles and watching him disappear headlong into the darkness. The fall was followed by a THUD and Stanley arrived on the floor in a heap.

'Er, sorry, lad. Me back gave way,' called MacDowell, poking his head through the opening. 'Can yer see owt?'

Stanley lit the stump of a candle in his pocket and the room came to life. Berkeley was not to be seen, and in the corner of the room the flag had been lifted again and the access to the mine had been exposed.

'Little devil!' Stanley snapped. 'Quick, come down here!'

The other two joined him, and all three

stared at the corner of the room.

'And how do you think he's done that?' gasped Stanley. 'I couldn't have lifted it in a million years and he's half my age and size.'

'Keep the noise down, Stanley. They're just above us,' whispered Daisy.

MacDowell scratched his chin and narrowed his eyes in thought.

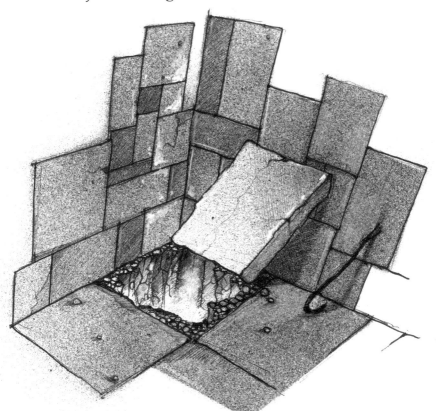

'Mmmmm.
Most of them are above us, Daisy, but I think
at least one of them is below. Come on,'
Stanley insisted. 'We need to find him.'

Down they went, back into the dank
blackness of the mine. MacDowell pulled out
more candle stumps from his pockets and
handed them round.

'I'll head this way,' he said, pointing straight
on. 'You two take these.' He indicated identical
tunnels that ran along either side. 'We'll meet
up at the far end, and if anybody gets hold o'
that little—'

'MAC!' said Daisy firmly. 'If we do find him,
we must be careful. He has just discovered the
greatest secret this island has, but he's a
little kid! Take it easy on him.'

'Aye, lass.
Yer right.' He clomped off through the
darkness, his head banging on the tunnel as
he went and his huge feet lolloping over the
stones. 'Ouch, ow, ouch!'

The three headed into the darkness alone.
The deeper they went, the colder and darker
it became. Daisy had suggested that as they
went along, they should leave large
drips of candle wax at shoulder
height along the rock. That
way, they could always
trace their way back.

Stanley's eyes opened
wide. He held the meagre
light from his candle up to
the walls and stared at the glittering gold.
It went on for ever.

The whole island
was one great big chunk of pirate treasure.

He stopped and looked in detail at
the bits of skull and bone that lay
embedded in the rock. Those too
went on for ever.

Every one of those skeletal pirates
had a ghastly tale to tell, no doubt.
Hundreds of years ago they must
have sailed a thousand miles just to
get here and dig in the mines. Many
a buccaneer's battle had been fought
down here and even now, in their death, they
still held on to each other's filthy stinking
bones in a brave attempt to win the treasure.

In the lowest points, the air was cooler still
and the walls still wet.

The odd crab scuttled out of the light as the
candle passed by, and harsh barnacles scraped
on Stanley's arms in the narrowest passages.

Stanley had to pinch himself: he had
become so carried away in what he was
seeing that he had forgotten his task. He was
searching for Berkeley, and time was of the
essence. Right now, one of the Darklings
might venture into the cellar and
uncover the raised flagstone.

Up ahead, Daisy could hear
something. A chinking sound,
almost as if someone was tapping
away at the rock that surrounded
them. It echoed through the tunnel,
which made it seem louder. Daisy held up
her candle and squinted

to sharpen her view. Nothing. She moved a little further on.

Every now and then the tunnels spilled out into big hollows with high ceilings. They formed little caves and then further on the way ahead disappeared into more small passageways.

Daisy wandered into one such cave and there in the distance, silhouetted by his candlelight, was Berkeley's unmistakable stubby frame.

She stood still and watched him. He was holding a small hammer and chisel and bashing away at the rock. Every now and then a small piece fell on to the floor, and he shoved it into a small cloth bag. He had stuck his candle on to a blob of wax on the wall so that his hands were free.

'The little—' began Daisy, but she was

stopped short when her own candle suddenly blew out in a draught.

The draught was caused by Stanley, racing up behind her as the ceiling opened out. He lifted his candle up to hers, and light returned.

MacDowell had lost his along the way. He came crawling out on hands and knees further ahead in the cave, and his sudden appearance startled Berkeley.

'Wallopin' whalebones, if it ain't the littlest pirate I ever saw, pinchin' the gold from old Davy Jones' locker. Come 'ere, yer little rat!' shouted MacDowell. Despite Daisy's good advice, he couldn't help himself and had blown his lid.

He scrambled to his feet and lunged at the small figure, but Berkeley was way too wick for old MacDowell and disappeared into the honeycombed trails ahead, without his candle.

'He won't get far without a light,' Daisy gasped, as they joined the race. But Stanley knew that the Darklings were used to the poor light that came with nocturnal living and if anyone could manage down here in the black, it was Berkeley.

The young Darkling whizzed through the tunnels, eager to escape. MacDowell was up front, and held up Daisy and Stanley. He had to stoop his long thin frame to stop himself banging his head, and his eyes were not as good as they used to be. Even though he didn't have a light, Berkeley was far quicker.

They reached a small cave and Stanley pushed past MacDowell, with Daisy hot on his heels.

But it was too late. As soon they'd discovered Berkeley, they'd lost him again.

And now, to make things worse, they had

lost their way. Rushing on, they hadn't taken
the time to mark their route with the candle
wax as Daisy had suggested.

The three of them stopped in their tracks.
They listened carefully and Berkeley's little
footsteps were still trotting through the
tunnels at an alarming rate. They couldn't tell
quite where the noise came from. It seemed to
echo all around them.

They had no choice; they had to find
him. They had already been down here for a
good while, but now they decided to stick
together. If only one of them became lost,
it would hold them *all* up. They took fresh
candles from their pockets.

Outside, waves were returning across the sand,
lapping at the dusty golden-yellow and washing
right over until it became a deep brown.

The sea came closer, and quickly, and before long a crashing wave of white foam filtered into a small crevice in the rock. Crabs and small creatures came with it, and climbed through the narrow rocky opening.

There were other slim openings in the rock, and the water washed inside until the deepest part of the smugglers' mine was already welcoming the return of the warm afternoon sea.

Desperation

The three friends had been in the mine so long that the light was starting to drop outside. But they didn't know that. They still envisaged the afternoon sun, with the villagers on the beach and the tide back. But the beach was gone now, out of sight until tomorrow.

Mrs Carelli looked out across the harbour from the gateway to the Hall.

Where were they now? Food was ready and laid out upon the table. She looked out at the purply-pale dusk that was awakening on the horizon and gently smothering the fading light.

But deep down, the searchers carried on. At times it seemed hopeless … but Stanley had found a small clue: freshly dug chunks of gold, dropped from Berkeley's cloth bag and giving away his trail. The candlelight picked out their presence as twinkles bounced back at them from the floor.

They followed the giveaway route, but it was working its way deeper and that was just what they didn't want.

There Berkeley was again, disappearing into the distance, looking over his shoulder as he went. But now water was washing

around their feet, and they knew what *that*
meant. Time was running out fast. Who knew
how far they had travelled, or how deep they
were? *They* certainly didn't.

They tried shouting out to him.

'Berkeley, stop! Berkeley, it's all right.
You're not in trouble, but we don't have long.
The tide's coming in!'

At first they thought he
was taking no notice, but
with some distance between
them he stopped up ahead
and looked round at them.

'What do you mean, the
tide's coming in?' his voice
echoed back to them. He
had a cross face and his
hands dug into his
pockets.

'Look, Berkeley, you're not in trouble! We need to get out of here. The tide will fill these tunnels with water before long, and we have to find the way back,' cried Daisy.

'You're lying. You just want my gold!' he sneered.

'Berkeley, we're not lying!' urged Stanley. 'We don't want your gold. If we don't find our way back, we'll all drown when the tide comes in.'

'Oh!' said Berkeley.

'Yes, OH! indeed, yer little bilge rat,' grumbled MacDowell. Stanley dug an elbow into his ribs to shut him up. 'Ooof, Stanley. That 'urt,' he complained.

'Good,' Stanley hissed. 'Now let's stick to the plan, please, Mac.'

'Berkeley, why don't you join us and we can find the way together. I bet you'd be

really good at showing us the way,' tried
Daisy in her most gentle tone.

'Don't want to. I like it down here,'
Berkeley said.

MacDowell was biting his lip in frustration.
He was ready to grab Berkeley by the throat
and drag him feet first through the mines.

Berkeley turned and ran again, into the
darkness. Or at least, he tried to. He had
gone a very short distance when he suddenly
found himself up to his waist in water. He
cried out, and the other three ran to
his aid. MacDowell's
long spindly
arms hoisted
him up out of
the foamy
water.

'I've dropped my bag. I've lost my gold!'
Berkeley cried.

'Never mind,' laughed MacDowell. 'Yer
look like a drowned moggy.'

Berkeley's legs kicked out at him.

'Calm down, young 'un, or I'll put yer back
in the wet, head first.'

Berkeley stopped immediately. He hated
the water, Stanley knew that – he'd seen him
run screaming at bath times when the family
had stayed at Candlestick.

'There's a good lad,' said MacDowell,
placing Berkeley gently on a rock and
holding a candle up to his face. 'Now listen.'

'Err … I'll do the talking, Mac,' insisted
Stanley. He began his explanation of why
they couldn't take any gold, because of what
it would mean to the island. Berkeley just
looked at him with a face as cross as he could

possibly make it. But under the circumstances, Stanley thought he had handled the news quite well. Maybe in the back of his mind, Berkeley knew he could return without them knowing at any time. Or so he thought. Stanley was already plotting to seal up the entrance hole from the Darkling cellar.

But only if they got out of there alive in the first place.

Both Mr and Mrs Carelli were out searching now. The light was fading fast, and there weren't many places left to look. They had been down to the candle shop, and searched the village. They knew for sure that the Hall was empty, and at this hour there was no way that they or anyone else was going to venture on to the moor, not with the return of you-know-what.

A fisherman made an early arrival at the
look-out post on the harbour, and reminded
Mrs Carelli that there was only an hour or so
left before complete darkness.

She was furious.

The Smugglers' Secret

*

Berkeley's recollection of his route was superbly accurate. Without even seeming to think he turned left and right, up and down. Like a soaking-wet sewer rat he trotted along, retracing his tracks.

Then suddenly he stopped and turned around.

'Stanley, I'll only show you the rest of the way if you promise to play with me when we get back,' he grinned.

'Berkeley, I'll play with you for the whole day tomorrow if you get us out of here. We'll take Steadman for a walk, we'll run on the beach, we'll go fishing, but please, pretty please, get us out of here fast. The water is coming up higher and we're still a long way from home.'

'You'll really play for the whole day?' he said, with a smile that ran from ear to ear.

'Yes, really,' said Stanley and he knew that he meant it because the thought of a normal day with a walk along the beach and a fishing trip and other such pleasures seemed like such a dream right now, even if he was to spend it with Berkeley.

They could hardly see as one by one their candles died and there were barely any stumps left to light. Stanley's stomach rumbled and he knew that a serious amount of time had now passed.

'Come on then,' said Berkeley, and he started to crawl through a tiny gap. Daisy and Stanley looked at each other, not believing that any of the rest of them would get through it. Only Berkeley had passed through this particular tunnel; everyone else had gone a different way. But they knew they had to stick to his route.

When Berkeley was through Daisy went next, but only just got through. Stanley was taller, but his wiry body was as thin as Berkeley's and out he popped.

Then came old MacDowell, huffing and puffing. He was built like a street lamp, but his pot belly got him into trouble.

The children pulled on his arms but he was well and truly stuck.

'Berkeley, where's your little stone chisel?' pleaded Stanley.

'Here,' Berkeley said, taking it and the hammer from his pocket.

Stanley set about chiselling away around MacDowell. The water was crashing in now, and really making a noise behind them.

"Urry!' cried MacDowell. 'It's up to me feet!'

'Don't worry,' Stanley replied through his teeth. 'Nearly there.'

But he couldn't help giggling at the
spectacle of MacDowell stuck by his belly,
and soon they all started. In fits of laughter
they pointed at MacDowell and their
cackling echoed round the tunnels.

'Shall we leave him there?' said Stanley.

'Yes, leave him!' grinned Berkeley, jumping
up and down.

'Just you wait till I get me 'ands on yer, yer skinny little—'

CRASH. A huge wave came rushing up behind MacDowell and loosened the crumbling rock around his belly. He came heaving down on the children and they were soaked in sea water. Only Daisy managed to keep her candle aloft, and now a single light was all they had to help them.

They jumped up quickly and pushed on.

Finally, they were in familiar territory. Stanley noticed the blobs of wax along the wall where they had started to leave their trace. But the water was up to their knees, and growing deeper.

But as they came to the last part of their journey, a dreadful realization dawned. The remaining network of tunnels was now completely submerged in water. And in the dark, it was impossible to find their way without drowning first.

Stanley turned round. The water that was up to his knees was almost up to Berkeley's chest.

But the young Darkling didn't panic. In a moment he was climbing higher into a new passage, leading upward.

'This way,' he called, and disappeared.

'Berkeley, wait … we don't even know if

we can get out that way,' cried Stanley.

But Berkeley was right: there was no other choice. They couldn't venture through a mine of tunnels submerged in water. And as the water rose beneath them, the only way was up. Up into the unknown. And so they followed.

They ventured this way and that, and though Berkeley had not been this way before he clearly had a sense of where he was. But as they moved upwards, so too did the water. It was as if they never made any progress. The water was always just beneath them.

They had gone a long way along a single tunnel when it led to a dead end.

'I guess that was going to happen eventually,' said Daisy.

'What?' asked Stanley.

'That we'd head the wrong way.'

'It's not the wrong way,' insisted Berkeley.

'It's just … it's just that there isn't a hole at the end to get out.'

'Oh, well that's all right then,' muttered MacDowell, holding his head in his hands.

Just then a trickle of water ran along the passage and circled around them as they sat hunched in the hole.

'It's here!' cried Berkeley. 'Now what?'

There was a stir of panic. Until now they'd had a feeling that Berkeley knew where he was going. But the water was quick to swill

around them and in moments it already had an uncomfortable depth to it.

Swiftly, they tried retracing their steps, but the route back was already filled with water.

This was it. The very last moment of their lives. MacDowell began to cry and the children comforted him.

'Sufferin' sea shells, I never thought I'd live me last moments under the drink,' he whimpered.

But Stanley looked at Daisy and through the last fading moments of candlelight their eyes met. Without even speaking, they had agreed not to give up the fight.

Stanley still had the hammer and chisel in his hands. It was worth a try.

He raised them above him and started to take small chunks of rock out of the ceiling of the tunnel.

To start with, it was a losing battle. As Stanley chipped away, loose pieces dropped into the water, raising its level – but, bit by bit, the space above them grew bigger.

'And what if we're still a mile below the surface?' panicked MacDowell. 'The water's getting higher.'

It was up to Berkeley's neck and he was raised up on his tiptoes.

'Hurry up, Stanley Buggles,' he cried, and a tear ran down his cheek. 'I don't like the water.'

Daisy hugged him tightly. 'Hang in there, Berkeley Darkling.' She too had a tear rolling down her cheek.

Stanley said nothing, concentrating all his efforts on the task at hand. He was sure he had heard the gulls harking above him. Perhaps they were closer to the surface than MacDowell had thought.

More clumps of rock fell down into the water. Stanley's arms ached.

"'Ere, lad, give us a try,' said MacDowell, but he was so long and wiry he couldn't lever his arms back to hit the hammer inside the small space.

Then Daisy tried. Chink, chink, chink. Little taps brought more small pieces down, but it seemed a hopeless task. MacDowell used the bits of rock to try and build up a dam against the water, but it poured through the tiniest gap.

Berkeley was still crying, with his head tilted back so that the water didn't run into his mouth.

'Stop blubbering,' said MacDowell. 'You're making more water.'

Stanley thought that was the most ridiculous and unhelpful thing anyone had ever said, but

he ignored it and held on to
Berkeley to reassure him.

Just then, a breakthrough.

'Look!' Stanley yelped.

'What is it?' they all cried in unison.

He pointed to a tiny thread of something
hanging from the ceiling.

'Stop, Daisy, stop,' he urged.

He yanked it free and held it up to them.

'It's a root, the end of a root, from a plant!
Here, Daisy, take a rest,' he insisted, and
began to bang away with renewed vigour.

'Hurry,' gasped Berkeley. 'Go faster.'
MacDowell was hoisting him up above the

level of the
water, but he couldn't
do that for long.

'Nearly there, little man,'
said Stanley. A smile broke
over his face as what he now knew was soil
began to drop into the water. He could smell
the fresh earthy smell of grass and plant life
on the black mud that swam around him.

Now instead of using the hammer and chisel
he was pulling away at clods of earth with his
hands. They all joined in, and Stanley's hand
was the first to spear through the soil into the
open air. He forced the space wider, then
shoved Berkeley up and out into freedom.

MacDowell grabbed Daisy and did the same for her, then Stanley. They forced the hole wider as they emerged and eventually the long bony shape of MacDowell grew out from the hole, popping his podgy belly through the opening.

'Sufferin' sea shells, Stanley. Yer sure know how to have an adventure, young lad, I'll give yer that one,' puffed MacDowell.

They sat a moment and got their bearings. They were out on the moor, in one of the lower-lying troughs. It was pitch black, and there were no more candles.

They stood up and brushed themselves down. Berkeley was shivering from head to toe and Daisy and Stanley hugged him tight to warm him.

Before they went anywhere, the four pushed and heaved a huge boulder over the hole they had just emerged from. No one would move *that* in a hurry.

And then something came across the air that reminded them just where they were. The distant howl of the wolf echoed over the Rock. With a good walk between themselves and home, and no weapon to beat the deadly threat that hung over the island, they set off into the night.

The Lupine Link

'Don't worry, Violet,' said Victor to Mrs Carelli, who was sitting in tears by the fireside. 'I'm sure they're safe. Old MacDowell is with them.'

'Oh, that clumsy old lummox. He can't even walk up the stairs without losing a leg through the balustrade. I've got more faith in the lad than I do in the brave pirate, that's for sure.'

The Smugglers' Secret

*

Meanwhile, as the four escapees walked gingerly out across the moor, Stanley and Daisy explained to Berkeley that no gold must ever leave the smugglers' mines. It would put the whole island in danger. Buccaneers would pull down the Darkling house just to get in there, and then they would destroy the Rock.

That was too much for Berkeley's pointy little ears. He burst into tears again as he held tightly on to Daisy's hand.

'I promise I'll never take another piece. I'll never go down there, not ever,' he insisted. 'Just as long as you promise you'll play with me.'

'Don't worry, Berkeley, when we've all had a good night's sleep we'll play with you,' agreed Stanley.

But he was barely listening. He had been in this situation before, out here on the moor in the dead of night, with the howl of the wolf echoing around him. At any moment it could spring on them, and he had no way of dealing with it.

Berkeley was completely at ease out on the dark moor. He skipped and trotted and ran among the rocks, disappearing here and there and jumping out on them with his eyes all aglow. But Stanley didn't see the funny side.

MacDowell was at their side, and cowered every time he heard a howl.

'Can yer tell the little wolf boy to stop his antics, Stanley? I'm worryin' meself 'alf to death ere.'

'Berkeley, please will you—' But no, he had gone again. Skipping off somewhere, only to jump out on them in a moment's time.

Stanley could hear him treading over old leaves up ahead, and he thought he'd surprise *him* this time, before Berkeley had the chance to surprise *them*.

But as he leaped around the corner, what stood before him wasn't Berkeley.

It was the formidable shape of the most fearsome creature on the Rock.

Stanley stepped back towards Daisy and old MacDowell. They stood huddled together, staring in shock, not able to move but wanting so desperately to run for their lives.

It all came back to Stanley: the filthy black shape, the coarse, hard coat that lay upon the huge arched back and the glowing eyes that seemed to hold them fixed right where they stood.

The grumbling low growl was meant for them, and Stanley was reminded that this horrible creature had already taken his good friend Phinn.

Saliva dribbled from its open mouth and it circled them warily.

Just then, the familiar shape of young Berkeley trotted around the corner. He had his eyes to the ground, not realizing that in the short moments that he had been off skipping around the rocks the others had put themselves in great danger.

Berkeley stopped and looked up.

The Smugglers' Secret

At first he could only see his three friends huddled together and motionless. And then in front of them, something else became clear.

What at first he had thought was the shape of a bush or tree was, on closer inspection, the pure black silhouette of the wolf.

Berkeley rushed forward, running in front of his three rescuers, desperate to protect them. He put himself between them and the hulking great black shape.

To everyone's great surprise, the wolf stepped back a touch as Berkeley moved in.

It looked hard into Berkeley's eyes, and he stared hard back at it.

'Go,' he said quietly.

In a wick twist and turn, the wolf moved around and was off into the night. It let out a pained howl of a cry as it thundered over the sweeping lows and highs of the Rock.

The group stared in astonishment at Berkeley. What power did he possess, to have such influence over this creature?

'How on earth did you *do* that, Berkeley?' begged Stanley.

'Do what?' Berkeley quizzed.

'You made it go away. That crazed beast was about to rip us to shreds, and you told it go, and it did. How on earth did you do that?' he persisted.

'I did nothing, Stanley. It was my father.'

Berkeley walked on with his head down as the cry of the wolf echoed over the moor.

Extending the alliance

The following day was split into two parts, and each part had its own dreaded task. The first: to sit and explain to Mr and Mrs Carelli, along with Lionel Grouse, Daisy's uncle, and Mrs Darkling, Berkeley's mother, about what had happened the previous day and why they were all missing until long after dark.

Stanley and Daisy sat and listened in

astonished disbelief at the tall tale that old
MacDowell spun without even batting an
eyelid. He was so convincing, Stanley almost
believed it himself. Berkeley
had been ordered to keep
his mouth shut firm and let
the bigger ones tell the
tale, but his comical
expressions questioned
MacDowell's every word.

The old buccaneer
weaved a long tale
about how they had
promised to treat
Berkeley to a day's fishing
and that they had all gone off
in a boat together and got lost. And by the
time they had found their way back it was
ever so late, but they had been safe all along,

and they even had the fish to prove it, but it had been left at the door in a panic when they heard the wolf, and the birds had been at it.

It was a good tale.

But not *that* good.

Mrs Carelli had lived on the Rock long enough to know that his little story didn't tie in with the tide times. Stanley was always up to something, that was to be expected, but she had a harsh view of MacDowell. He had lied to her too convincingly, and all her suspicions were aroused. She wondered if perhaps he was still up to his old pirate tricks.

For the moment, she pushed her doubts aside.

The second task of the day was slightly harder. Stanley reminded MacDowell that the stone slab in Berkeley's cellar needed replacing. It was foolish to have left it open like that for so long. Stanley had decided he trusted Berkeley, but the temptation would not be good for him.

Berkeley had reluctantly agreed to go along with the plan. 'But Stanley, you said you'd play with me today,' he moaned.

'Berkeley, I promise you that once we have tied up all these odds and ends we will play.'

'Is that a *real* promise?' Berkeley pushed.

'More real than you could possibly imagine,' Stanley insisted, and he held out his hand to plant a firm grip of confirmation upon his young friend.

Berkeley was to get his family out of the house under the pretence that they should take a family walk and try to forget their worries for the afternoon.

Mrs Darkling was proud of her son. How

thoughtful of him to be concerned about his mother and the well-being of his siblings!

They trotted along the harbour in a long line. Mrs Darkling was at the front, followed by Annabelle, the eldest daughter, then Olive, Berkeley's twin sister, and then at the back was Berkeley himself. Steadman trotted behind with his head held low, sniffing here and there and dragging rubbish out from the waste bins.

And at the same time, heading the other way towards the Darkling place, were MacDowell, Stanley and Daisy. In a routine movement that had become all too familiar, they stole inside the Darkling cellar – from the strength of the midday sun to the damp,

cool darkness below ground.

Inside, the cellar was untouched, with the flagstone lifted in the corner. Quite how Berkeley had lifted it the last time, they couldn't work out. Perhaps his father had been in on the act with Berkeley and he hadn't said. In all that had happened, Stanley had forgotten to ask him.

Below, they could hear the sea crashing against the Rock. The tide was retreating again, and they were able to stare down into the space below, one last time.

Then the stone flag was lowered down into position and cemented at the edges, and now the smugglers' mine was sealed.

Peace of mind was already returning for Stanley. He had made amends with Berkeley, and they had learned to trust one another through their trials and tribulations.

But as the three conspirators left the Darkling cellar for the last time, the smugglers' mine was still under threat of more exposure. Berkeley was being hounded by his sisters while Mrs Darkling wandered on to the moor with Steadman.

'We know where you went yesterday, Berkeley,' grinned Annabelle. Her expression disturbed him slightly.

'No you don't,' he said.

'Yes we do,' continued Olive. 'You disappeared down the little rabbit hole.'

'It isn't a rabbit hole.'

'Yes it is, Berkeley. You've got a cute little
rabbit and that's where you keep it!' laughed
Olive.

'No I haven't. It's a gold mine, with treasure,
and dead pirates and … oh!' He began to cry.
He had already broken his
promise to Stanley
about keeping
his mouth
shut.

The girls laughed.

'It's all right, Berkeley. We've already seen it. We won't tell anyone your little secret. When Mother sent us to find you, we saw the entrance to your little cave and we went inside,' explained Olive.

'We only came back because the water was too deep,' said Annabelle. 'We'd like to take another look.'

'Absolutely *not*,' came a voice over their shoulders. It was Stanley, accompanied by Daisy and MacDowell.

'All done,' he said, nodding to Berkeley.

He'd had a feeling that the mine might have been found by the Darkling girls. It made sense that they would have looked all over the place for Berkeley, the previous day, and now Stanley was forced to allow the girls into the secret alliance.

They were an elite group, held together by the fact that they were the only ones who knew the great secret of the Rock. No matter what they thought of one another, they had to agree that they would not let the secret out. It was for the good of the Rock, and for the safety of everyone, especially the Darklings, whose home made the entrance to the mines.

When Olive and Annabelle heard it explained to them like this, their faces changed.

It was no longer a secret to taunt Berkeley with, it was their whole way of life that lay in danger. Not only the place they knew as home, but life on the Rock. They could never be anywhere else.

They stood in the square and held hands around the water fountain to form a ring.

Taking it in turns, they each made a solemn promise to keep the secret to themselves and protect the future of the Rock.

The Turn-coat

Mrs Carelli looked out from the lounge window. She was watching Stanley and Daisy running along the beach with the Darkling children, while Steadman trotted eagerly behind.

'He's got in with a bad lot,' said Mrs Carelli. 'I don't like it, Victor.'

'Ah, leave them be,' said Victor. 'They're

only playing.' He was far more diplomatic than Mrs Carelli and whenever he showed such a reaction it always made her think twice. Was she being unnecessarily harsh? Perhaps so!

But little did they know that the five children, along with MacDowell (and Steadman of course), had formed what they called the Secret-Keepers Alliance, and each of them (apart from Steadman) had promised to hold the secret close and never tell another living soul. And that way, the great secret of Crampton Rock would never leak out.

Stanley and Daisy sat together on the harbour wall. The Darkling children were running along the sand and MacDowell was being chased by Steadman. The dog hadn't left him alone all afternoon.

'I think that MacDowell's bony legs get Steadman's appetite going,' remarked Stanley as they watched them flying past along the beach.

'It's like me or you having to stare closely at one of Mrs Carelli's pies!'

Daisy laughed. She loved Stanley's way of always being able to make something funny.

But she couldn't help being serious.

'Everything has changed. Our secret feels like public knowledge, Stanley. Suddenly, there are six of us. And what worries me is that we barely know the others.'

'I know,' Stanley started. 'I feel the same, Daisy, I really do. But they barely know us either. We are all trusting each other.

We were eager to get to the spot on the map, and I guess it landed us in a whole new mess with a brand-new set of problems. It was just an accident that we all ended up in it together, but I guess we all have one thing in common.'

'Which is?' she said, gazing up at him.

'We all want things to stay as they are, Daisy. We all love it here, and we're happy.'

'But what about Edmund Darkling?' Daisy exclaimed. 'He's still at large, hiding out in the day and at night putting the whole place under threat. What about that? He's the father to three of the people in the Secret-Keepers Alliance!'

'I know, Daisy but what can we do? We can only live with the situation. But one thing is for sure,' Stanley proclaimed. 'When I first came here there was a werewolf at large.

It kept this place quiet. It stopped pirates from arriving here and snooping around. It kept everyone indoors at night, especially those who might be up to no good, and it was the best form of security this place could possibly have had. So if there is such thing as a good situation out of a bad one, then this might be a good example of it.'

'But the Darkling children plotted to kill you!' cried Daisy.

'Not *really*,' said Stanley. 'They were forced into believing that their father's way of thinking was right, that's all!'

Daisy looked unsure, so Stanley persisted. 'Deep down, I don't think they're so bad. I know it sounds crazy, but I think they were just doing as they were told. They have had a strange and severe upbringing. And whilst we're here, do we make them into enemies or friends? Considering what they know, believe me, Daisy, we are better off as friends!'

Daisy knew he was right. However daft and clumsy Stanley was at times, deep down there was a good head on those shoulders.

The next day, the five children found themselves in the same spot. The sea was right up against the harbour wall as early evening arrived and the lamps were lit across the seafront. A group of fishermen were huddling around a fire basket.

The children sat talking, and Stanley remembered something he had been meaning to ask Berkeley.

'Berkeley, tell me one thing,' began Stanley as the whole group listened in.

Berkeley walked towards Stanley along the harbour wall.

'Yes, Stanley, what is it?' he grinned.

'How on earth did you lift that slab of stone in the cellar? It's had me baffled for some time. I know you're a strong little fellow, but those stones are huge. What did you do to lift it?'

'Nothing!' insisted Berkeley.

'What do you mean, nothing?' pushed Stanley.

'I mean, I didn't do anything. It was already like that when I went down there,' he said, shrugging his shoulders.

'But we put it back, Daisy, didn't we? We put it back! I know we did. No one could possibly say we didn't put it back. I remember it so clearly,' Stanley insisted.

Just then, Daisy nudged Stanley and pointed him in the direction of a boat that was bobbing and swaying on the surf as it waited in the harbour. Someone was loading their things into the cabin.

'It's Mister Mac!' said Berkeley.

And sure enough it was. Old MacDowell was packing his things into the boat. They wandered across and sat on the harbour in front of the small boat.

'Mac, what are you doing?' called Stanley. 'This isn't your boat!'

'Ahh, Stanley. Yer caught me red-'anded, lad. I'm leavin' the Rock, so I am.'

'LEAVING?' they yelled.

'I'm sorry, kids,' he began. 'I ain't cut out for all this any more. My days o' wild adventures is over. I'm none too keen on the thought o' werewolves wanderin' around at night. I'm planning on livin' a little bit longer, if yer know what I'm sayin'.'

'But you're part of the alliance!' said Stanley.

'You can't leave here now. I thought you were happy at the Hall.'

'Stanley, don't get me wrong, I appreciate yer hospitality an' all that but I never intended stayin' for ever. I like to move on now and again.'

'Well at least let us help you with your things,' said Stanley.

'No, please. I'm fine,' MacDowell insisted, but Stanley had already interfered. He picked up a large case. It was so heavy that as he lifted it across, it fell out of his hands and its contents spilled across the bottom of the boat.

A thousand little pieces of golden rock showered the wooden carcass of the boat. They shone and twinkled in the moonlight that had begun to spill across the seafront.

All the children gasped. MacDowell looked awkwardly at Stanley, not wanting to meet his eye.

'Awww, come on, Stanley,' he said. 'It's only a couple o' pieces.'

'But you've broken the alliance!' exclaimed Stanley, his jaw dropping wide open.

'No I ain't, 'cause I ain't told nobody else!' MacDowell insisted.

'We agreed!' said Daisy. 'We agreed that none of us would take a single piece.'

'I ain't pinchin' from nobody, am I? Same as if I grabbed a couple o' shells off the beach there. Don't belong to no one. Belong to whoever picks 'em up an' takes 'em, just like you said, Stanley.'

Berkeley was furious. He jumped into the boat and bit MacDowell's left leg, sending him hopping around the deck.

'Aargh, yer little devil. Where on earth did yer get teeth as sharp as that?' MacDowell yelled, as the children sneered and giggled at him.

He stood up straight and tried to compose himself.

Stanley was still staring hard at him, absolutely infuriated.

'Mac, when you came here you were looking for my Great-Uncle Bart. I've let you stay at the Hall all this time. I think we deserve a proper explanation,' he insisted.

'Ahh, I 'ave to be straight with yer, Stanley. Yer a good kid and I like yer, but I weren't never no friend o' Bart Swift. I never knew yer great-uncle. I only came 'ere for what's in that bag,' he admitted.

Stanley's frown deepened. 'But what about all the tales of pirate days and wild adventures with my great-uncle?'

'Ahh, I always told a good tale, lad. But that's 'ow I got yer out o' that mess the other day, now isn't it?' he muttered, almost as if he had done Stanley a huge favour.

'It was you!' said Stanley as he realized. '*You* went back to the mines when we weren't there and took out the gold. And then you forgot to replace the stone slab in the corner. We couldn't understand how Berkeley had lifted it, but he didn't. He said he didn't and he was telling the truth. It was you. You're just a villain!'

'Once a pirate, always a pirate, eh lad? It'll be a long time afore old MacDowell gives up on gold, I tell you. And I guess I'll be back for more. But don't worry, I'll keep a lid on it. Mum's the word!' he said. 'I told yer I wouldn't break me promise. I won't tell no one.'

He lifted the rope that held his boat to the harbour, hoisted his little white sail and picked up all his golden nuggets, tucking them safely back into the case.

And then, as the five remaining members of the Secret-Keepers Alliance watched from the quayside, the silhouette of old MacDowell sailed off alone into the evening sunset, with the waves lapping behind him.

'Can we play now?' asked Berkeley.

Stanley stared at Berkeley's forlorn little face and gave a long hard sigh.

'Race you to the house!' he said, and the two of them clattered across the cobbles up to the door of Candlestick Hall.

Scribbles from the

Something Wickedly Weird

sketchbook

Chris Mould went to art school at the age of sixteen. During this time, he did various jobs, from delivering papers to washing up and cooking in a kitchen. He has won the Nottingham Children's Book Award and been commended for the Sheffield. He loves his work and likes to write and draw the kind of books that he would have liked to have on his shelf as a boy. He is married with two children and lives in Yorkshire.

Crampton Rock seems the perfect place to spend a long summer holiday. But there's always something to go and spoil it all, isn't there?

Why are all the dogs three-legged? Is there really a **werewolf** on the loose? And what do the *pirates* want with Stanley Buggles...?

SOMETHING WICKEDLY WEIRD

The Werewolf and the Ibis

CHRIS MOULD

All looks crisp and cosy in
Crampton Rock as Stanley Buggles
settles down for the winter.
But something wicked has blown
in with the wind.

What is the **headless ghost**
of Admiral Swift desperate to tell Stanley?

And who are the *deadly pirates*,
marching through the oncoming blizzard ...?

SOMETHING
WICKEDLY
WEIRD

The Ice Pirates

CHRIS MOULD

Up ahead, the shape of **Crampton Rock** grows clear through the misty glass of a hundred telescopes. The black pirate swarm moves ever closer for the final battle.

What has awoken the **skeletons** from their slumber? And how can Stanley Buggles *escape* from their deadly grip ...?

SOMETHING WICKEDLY WEIRD
The Buccaneer's Bones

CHRIS MOULD

The island of **Crampton Rock** has emerged from **pirate battle**. But something far more sinister is on the move...

What claim does the **Darkling family** have on Stanley Buggles' home?

And do the Darkling twins really keep a **two-headed snake** as a pet?

SOMETHING WICKEDLY WEIRD

The Curse of the Wolf

CHRIS MOULD

With a werewolf still on the loose, Stanley Buggles knows that **Crampton Rock** lies in **deadly danger.**

Who will confront the **escaped** criminal roaming the wild and windy moor?

And how will the **treasure keepers** protect the gold mine from the **threat of piracy** ...?

Are you prepared to be scared?

This book contains ten of the most terrifying tales, adapted, written and superbly illustrated by award-winner

Chris Mould.

Five are original ghost stories, and five are retellings of classic tales, from *The Legend of Sleepy Hollow* by Washington Irving to *The Tell-Tale Heart* by Edgar Allen Poe.

Open this book at your own peril ...